Walt Disney's
Alice in Wonderland

Senior Designer: Elaine Lopez
Editor: Sharon Yates
Editorial Director: Pamela Pia

Walt Disney's
Alice in Wonderland

Illustrations by The Walt Disney Studios

Illustrations adapted by
Al Dempster

Reader's
Digest
Children's Books™

Pleasantville, New York • Montréal, Québec • Bath, United Kingdom

Alice was growing tired, listening to her sister read. Just as her eyes began to close, she saw a white rabbit hurry by.

The white rabbit was looking at his pocket watch
and talking to himself. Alice thought that was very
curious indeed — a talking rabbit with a pocket watch!
So she followed him into a rabbit hole beneath a big tree.

And down she fell, down to the center of the world, it seemed.

When Alice landed with a thump, the White Rabbit was just disappearing through a door, which was much too small for her.

Alice drank from a bottle on the table and shrank
down to a very tiny size. But now she could not reach
the key to the little door!

DRINK
ME

At last, Alice found a way to get through the little
door. Seated on a bottle, she floated into Wonderland
on a mysterious sea.

On the shore of the Wonderland Sea, Alice joined a race.
It had no beginning; it had no end — you just ran around
and around.

On through Wonderland Alice went, in search of the White Rabbit. She met two jolly fellows, Tweedledum and Tweedledee.

They did not know the rabbit, but they told Alice
a wonderful story about a walrus and a carpenter who
walked beside the sea.

Alice listened politely. Then she hurried on. And finally, at a neat little house in the woods, she met the White Rabbit himself! The rabbit sent Alice into his little house to hunt for his gloves. But instead she found some cookies labeled TAKE ONE. So she did.

The cookie made Alice grow as big as the house! The White Rabbit and his friend Dodo thought she was a dreadful monster. Alice picked a carrot from the rabbit's garden. Eating it made her small again — so small that she was soon lost in a forest of grass.

Soon Alice found herself in a garden of live, talking flowers. There were bread-and-butterflies and rocking-horseflies, too. Alice thought the garden was a pleasant place. But the flowers thought Alice was just a weed, so they would not let her stay.

Next, Alice met a haughty caterpillar. He told her to eat the mushroom that he was sitting on if she wished to change her size.

Alice sampled one side of the mushroom and shot up taller than the treetops, frightening the birds. But another bite made her just the right size.

"Now, which way shall I go?" Alice wondered. The signposts she found along the path were no help — they pointed in every direction.

"If I were looking for the White Rabbit, I'd ask the Mad Hatter," said a grinning Cheshire Cat up in a tree. "He lives down there."

Alice found the Mad Hatter and the March Hare celebrating their un-birthdays at a tea party. She joined them for a while.

After that nonsensical tea party, Alice wanted to go home.
But none of the strange creatures she met seemed to know
the way.

Alice wandered into the Queen's Garden. But the gardeners could not help her. They were all busy as could be, painting the roses red. Then along came the Royal Procession. And who should be the royal trumpeter for the Queen of Hearts but the White Rabbit himself!

The Queen asked Alice to play croquet. But Alice did not like the looks of the game. "Off with her head!" cried the Queen. Away Alice ran, while the army of cards chased her, down all the tangled paths of Wonderland, and back to the riverbank.

"I'm glad to be back where things are really what they seem," said Alice as she woke up from her strange Wonderland dream.